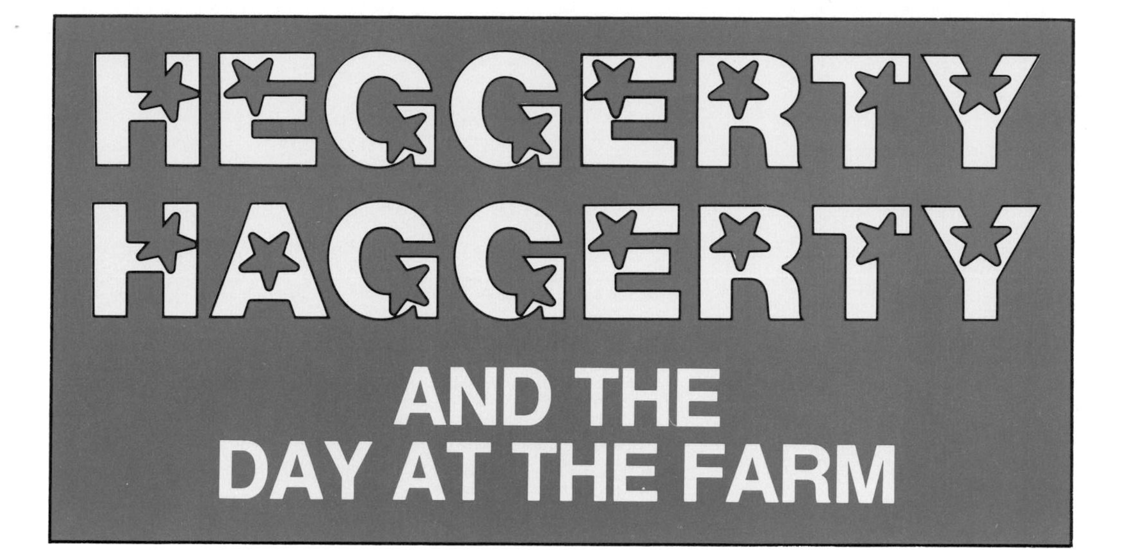

Stories by Elizabeth Lindsay
Pictures by Peter Rush

Hippo Books
Scholastic Book Services
London

For Ryan

Scholastic Book Services Inc.,
10 Earlham Street, London WC2H 9LN

Scholastic Inc.,
730 Broadway, New York, NY 10003, USA

Scholastic Tab Publications Ltd.,
123 Newkirk Road, Richmond Hill,
Ontario L4C 3G5, Canada

Ashton Scholastic Pty. Ltd., P.O. Box 579, Gosford,
New South Wales, Australia

Ashton Scholastic Ltd., 165 Marua Road,
Panmure, Auckland, New Zealand

First published in the UK by Scholastic Book Services Inc., 1985

ISBN 0 590 70438 9

Typeset in Plantin by Keyline Graphics Ltd, London NW6

It was a sunny September morning with a nip in the air. Broomstick was washing up the breakfast things when there was a knock at the front door.

"I'll go," said Broomstick. Mr Jones the postman stood on the doorstep. "I thought I'd knock just to tell you that Farmer Giles has got the 'flu. He ought to be tucked up in bed, if you ask me," said Mr Jones.

"Thank you for telling me, Mr Jones. We'll go down and see him at once," said Heggerty Haggerty.

She started getting things ready straight away.

"We'll need to take some of my special influenza medicine; some of that nice tomato soup I made; a hot-water bottle and some apples."

"Why apples?" asked Broomstick.

"Because an apple a day keeps the doctor away. We'll tuck him up in bed and get on with the farm work ourselves."

Heggerty Haggerty filled her basket and fetched her *Book of Spells* from behind the grandfather clock.

"Just in case," she said. "Coming Blackcat?"

Heggerty Haggerty and Blackcat climbed aboard Broomstick's back and he flew down the hill to the farm.

They found Farmer Giles in the cowshed milking Abigail, his favourite black-and-white cow. He looked pale and was shivering.

"Tut, tut," said Heggerty Haggerty. "This will not do."

"We've come to help out so you can go to bed," said Broomstick.

"That's very kind of you," said Farmer Giles with a sniff. He blinked as tears came into his eyes. "Very kind."

"That's what friends are for," said Heggerty Haggerty.

In the farmhouse, Farmer Giles went upstairs to put on his pyjamas and get into bed. Heggerty Haggerty boiled the kettle for the hot-water bottles and warmed the tomato soup in a pan. The apples she put in the oven to bake.

"I'll make some custard later," she said.

Blackcat watched as Heggerty Haggerty filled first Farmer Giles' hot-water bottle and then the one she had brought from home.

"That means Farmer Giles will have one for his front, one for his back but what about his toes?" thought Blackcat.

Farmer Giles was sitting up in bed. He was shivering all over. Blackcat jumped onto the bed with a purr. He nosed his way between the sheets and wriggled down the bed to Farmer Giles' toes.

He curled his warm furry body around them. Goodness they were cold. Despite his shivering, Farmer Giles' face broke into a smile.

Heggerty Haggerty came upstairs carrying a large tray on which was the medicine, the steaming tomato soup and the hot-water bottles. Farmer Giles tucked one hot-water bottle behind him and rested the other on his tummy.

He opened his mouth wide as Heggerty Haggerty slipped in a spoonful of her special influenza medicine.

Then he sipped some tomato soup to take the taste away.

"We'll soon have you well again," said Heggerty Haggerty. "Now tell me what needs doing on the farm."

"Well, I was going to plough the bottom field."

"Splendid," said Heggerty Haggerty. "Broomstick and I will enjoy doing that."

"What are we going to do?" asked Broomstick.

"We're going to plough the bottom field."

The tractor and the plough were in the barn. They hitched the plough on the back of the tractor and Heggerty Haggerty got onto the driver's seat. She started the engine and the tractor roared into life.

"You go ahead and open the gates," shouted Heggerty Haggerty. Broomstick flew and opened the gate to the first field. The tractor came shooting out of the barn, past the gate and stopped in front of the kitchen door.

Heggerty Haggerty looked flustered.

She pulled hard on the steering wheel.

It charged through the gate missing Broomstick by a hair's breadth.

"I'm getting the hang of it," called Heggerty Haggerty.

Broomstick flew down the field and opened the bottom gate. Heggerty Haggerty drove through it.

"Lower the plough, please, Broomstick," she called. Broomstick lowered the plough. Heggerty Haggerty drove off. The plough followed behind the tractor turning the earth into rich brown furrows. The only problem was that the furrows weaved this way and that. Heggerty Haggerty was not driving straight.

"This is hopeless," said Broomstick.

Broomstick flew to the farmhouse for the *Book of Spells* as fast as he could. When he came back he hid behind the hedge and said:

"Please, book, a ploughing recipe as quickly as you can."

The *Book of Spells* opened in his hands and he read, "Ploughing made easy. Recipe for."

Broomstick looked carefully at what he had to do. There were some special magic movements and some special magic whistles. He practised the whistles for a bit. It was words first, wave the arms, whistle the whistles and more words.

"Here goes," he said and began.

Meanwhile, in the field the tractor was bumping Heggerty Haggerty up and down for all it was worth. She was getting very fed up.

"This is ridiculous," she said. "I'm not getting any better at straight lines and I've been practising for ages. There's something wrong with this tractor. It's not behaving as it should." At these words the tractor gave a sudden lurch. Heggerty Haggerty clung on. She was half out of her seat.

"What is the matter with this machine?" she cried. The bumping seemed to get even worse. Heggerty Haggerty looked up and saw Broomstick hovering above.

"It's all right," he said. "I've magiced it."

"You've what? When?" asked Heggerty Haggerty.

"Just now. Watch out!"

The tractor gave an enormous leap which tossed Heggerty Haggerty into the air. Broomstick caught her and sat her on his back.

"I just thought it might do it better with a bit of magic," he said.

Heggerty Haggerty looked down at the field. The ploughing she had done was very higgledy piggledy and lots of bits were missed

"I suppose it is a good idea," she sighed. "That tractor is a menace. I don't know how Farmer Giles managed it."

"He's used to it and you're not," said Broomstick comfortingly. "And wouldn't it be terrible if Farmer Giles had to do it all again."

Heggerty Haggerty agreed. "It would."

They watched as the tractor drove itself to the edge of the field and began the ploughing again. The earth was turned furrow next to furrow just as it should be.

"Very nice indeed," said Heggerty Haggerty. "While it's doing that, let's go and have a baked apple. They should be ready now."

They collected the *Book of Spells* from the top of the gatepost where Broomstick had left it and flew back to the farmhouse.

The tractor seemed to watch them go because as soon as they were out of sight the engine opened up and it began ploughing at twice the speed. Soon it had finished the field. But instead of stopping it drove out of the gate, into the lane, and set off down the road towards the village.

A little while later when Heggerty Haggerty and Broomstick flew down the hill, feeling comfortably full of baked apples and custard, they were surprised to find the tractor gone.

"Oh, no," said Heggerty Haggerty in alarm. "What's it up to?"

They followed the trail of mud the tractor wheels had laid. They could hear, in the distance, the chug chugging of a tractor engine.

When they arrived at the village green they could not believe their eyes. The tractor was busy ploughing up every bit of grass it could find.

"Quick, Broomstick," cried Heggerty Haggerty.

Broomstick swooped down to the tractor. Heggerty Haggerty clicked her fingers and muttered a spell. The engine spluttered and stopped.

"Well, well, well, what's going on here then?" asked Constable Short, who had just arrived on the scene. He stood tall and stern and took out his notebook. The villagers crowded round to see what happened.

"Is this your tractor, Heggerty Haggerty?" Constable Short asked

Heggerty Haggerty was pink with embarrassment. She looked at the ploughed-up village green and decided magic was the only answer. She did a quick "as you once were" recipe with her fingers whispering to herself the words:

"FOLD AWAY FOLD BACK
BE AS YOU WERE
TURN INTO GRASS AGAIN
WITHOUT A STIR,"

and the earth turned over and was grass again. Constable Short's eyes nearly popped out of his head.

"Well, well, fancy that," he said and put away his notebook. "Perhaps you wouldn't mind moving this obstruction." He pointed to the tractor.

Heggerty Haggerty was only too pleased to and drove the tractor back to the farm and parked it in the barn.

Farmer Giles had a good chuckle when they told him what had happened. He was feeling a lot better.

"That's a good story," he grinned. "I'm feeling much more like my old self. Thank you for looking after me." Blackcat came out from under the sheets and gave a purr. Farmer Giles tickled his ears. Heggerty Haggerty's special influenza medicine had done the trick!

PRINTED IN BELGIUM BY proost INTERNATIONAL BOOK PRODUCTION